PIRATE'S TREASURE

By Maria S. Barbo
Illustrated by Duendes del Sur

ABDOPUBLISHING.COM

Reinforced library bound edition published in 2017 by Spotlight, a division of ABDO. PO Box 398166, Minneapolis, Minnesota 55439. Spotlight produces high-quality reinforced library bound editions for schools and libraries. Published by agreement with Warner Bros. Entertainment Inc.

Printed in the United States of America, North Mankato, Minnesota.
042016   092016

THIS BOOK CONTAINS
RECYCLED MATERIALS

PUBLISHER'S CATALOGING IN PUBLICATION DATA

Names: Barbo, Maria S., author. | Duendes del Sur, illustrator.
Title: Scooby-Doo and the pirate's treasure / by Maria S. Barbo ; illustrated by Duendes del Sur.
Description: Minneapolis, MN : Spotlight, [2017] | Series: Scooby-Doo early reading adventures
Summary: The Mystery, Inc. gang is going on a treasure hunt when Scooby disappears. Did a pirate ghost take him? It's up to the gang to solve the mystery and find Scooby!
Identifiers: LCCN 2016930652 | ISBN 9781614794714 (lib. bdg.)
Subjects: LCSH: Scooby-Doo (Fictitious character)--Juvenile fiction. | Dogs--Juvenile fiction. | Pirates--Juvenile fiction. | Ghosts--Juvenile fiction. | Treasure troves--Juvenile fiction. | Mystery and detective stories--Juvenile fiction. | Adventure and adventurers--Juvenile fiction.
Classification: DDC [Fic]--dc23
LC record available at http://lccn.loc.gov/2016930652

Spotlight
A Division of ABDO
abdopublishing.com

Scooby and the gang were
having a picnic in the park.
Scooby and Shaggy were eating
sandwiches.
Velma was reading a book.
Fred and Daphne were playing
Frisbee.

"According to this book, there's a pirate's treasure in this park," said Velma. "Old legend says the ghost of a pirate watches over it."

"Ghost?" asked Shaggy.

"Rhost?" yelped Scooby.

Scooby hid under the picnic basket.

Just then, they heard a loud, buzzing sound nearby.

Bzzzzzz.

Fred and Daphne were curious about Velma's book.

"I wonder if we can find the pirate's treasure," said Velma.

"Like, I wonder if there's honey in that beehive," said Shaggy.

Scooby smelled the honey and he went to investigate.

"Mmmm," said Scooby, tasting the honey.

The bees did not like Scooby tasting their honey.

And they did not like Scooby taking their beehive.

Bzzzzzzzzzzzzzz went the bees as they chased Scooby out of the park.

Fred was busy making plans to look for the pirate's treasure.

"There's a map in Velma's book," said Fred. "We should go on a treasure hunt."

"Like, does anyone know where Scooby went?" asked Shaggy.

"Uh-oh," said Velma. "We better find Scooby."

Scooby was running with the beehive through the trees.

The bees were buzzing after him.

Scooby ran up a tree.

He bumped into some baby birds in a nest.

The baby birds' parents were not happy to find Scooby with their nest on his head.

Then the bees caught up to Scooby and he was on the run again.

"Scooby, where are you?" called Velma.

Velma and Shaggy looked for Scooby in the park.

They found some honey on the trees.

"The ghost of the pirate treasure was here!" said Shaggy.

The bees and the birds chased Scooby past some kids flying kites.

Scooby had the bird's nest on his head and the beehive in his paws.

The birds were hot on his tail and the bees were close behind. Scooby was scared.

Fred and Daphne kept looking for Scooby in the park.

"Scooby, where are you?" called Daphne. "I have Scooby-Snacks for you."

They found a group of very unhappy kids.

"Our kites are covered in honey!" one boy cried.

"Sorry about your kites," said Fred to the kids. "I think we're getting closer to finding Scooby," he told the gang.

Scooby was a mess. A kite was covering his eyes and he ran right into a tree.

The birds pecked at Scooby's head and the bees buzzed in his ears.

"Relp!" Scooby shouted.

"Scoob, where are you?" called Shaggy.

Velma found honey on a tree near the lake.

"Why is there honey everywhere we go?" asked Velma.

Then she saw some bees buzzing nearby.

"Look!" Fred yelled. Everyone turned and saw Scooby in the lake. "Scooby found the Pirate's Treasure," said Velma. "It's a waterslide!"

"Like, I'm sure glad there's no pirate ghost," said Shaggy.

Scooby had found new homes for the bees and the birds too.

"Good job, Scooby," Daphne said.

"Scooby-Dooby-Doo!" barked Scooby.

The End